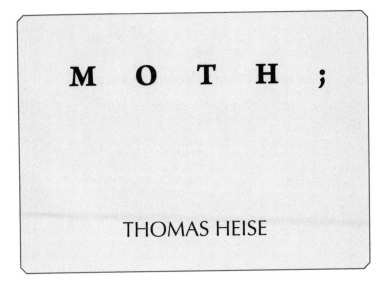

M O T H ;

THOMAS HEISE

SARABANDE BOOKS
LOUISVILLE, KENTUCKY

or how I came to be with you again

for my mother and Ms. M.

© 2013 by Thomas Heise

FIRST EDITION

Managing Editor
Sarabande Books, Inc.
2234 Dundee Road, Suite 200
Louisville, KY 40205

Library of Congress Cataloging-in-Publication Data

Heise, Thomas.
Moth; or how I came to be with you again / Thomas Heise.
  pages cm
ISBN 978-1-936747-57-3 (pbk. : alk. paper)
I. Title.
PS3608.E385M88 2013
811'.6—dc23

2012049322

Cover and text design by Kirkby Gann Tittle.

Manufactured in Canada.

This book is printed on acid-free paper.

Sarabande Books is a nonprofit literary organization.

This project is supported in part by an award from the National Endowment for the Arts.

The Kentucky Arts Council, the state arts agency, supports Sarabande Books with state tax dollars and federal funding from the National Endowment for the Arts.

moth: [m θ] *n.* Any of numerous, nocturnal insects of the order *Lepidoptera* that are attracted to light, excluding butterflies.

Related: **moth•er:** *n.* One who watches, pursues, captures, and collects moths. *See also:* **mother.**

Lepidoptera — Graellsia isabellae — Spanish Moon Moth

I am sad, not because you are leaving, but because I am going to forget you.

—Proust

Whatever is conscious wears out. Whatever is unconscious remains unalterable. Once freed, however, surely this too must fall to ruins.

—Freud

she was so bright

      no one loved her

   like the moth

A Note

At some point in the winter of 2009, I became aware that I have been afflicted for years with a strange, unclassified condition that makes my experience of time markedly different from that of others. I hesitate to use the word "illness," since there is nothing pathogenic about which I write, the viral properties of language itself notwithstanding. The river of my memory, my own past and that odd concept we call the present, which is ever in the process of being added to the detritus that is by common agreement a sign of life, flows in many directions.

I have always had a hazy understanding of my own history—who my parents were, where I have come from, where I am returning to—but in the months that I was under the care of Drs. T.W., F.W., and T.R., I was told that the liminal region between what was real and what was not had become for me indistinguishable, a mere phantom. All evidence to the contrary, I did not know whether to believe them for they took such an unusual interest in my case that at times I wondered if they might not be diagnosing themselves. As I stared up at their faces leaning over the bed those days that blurred into weeks before my release last season, they often had the look of those who gaze for too long into the pond of Monet's water lilies.

Days of sleeping alternated with spells of insomnia, which were interrupted by periods when I did not know if I were awake or dreaming because the images and ideas that appeared in my mind were often so unfamiliar that I half-suspected they were beamed in as a radio signal from a distant shore, or emerged up out of a seabed of a primordial life I had once lived, had all but forgotten, and whose vestiges on occasion made themselves known. I became lost in time and, in retrospect, lost in words. The moments of involuntary recall during which the unrecoverable past piling up behind me were only matched by the expansive fields of time that even now remain barren in my memory. Fortunately, I am told that the rubble will wear down to a fine, particulate mist that the winds of the imagination will scatter, like the storm blowing in from Paradise for Benjamin's Angel who cannot close its wings.

Was my life now a second life and was my life in writing a third, I simply do not know. Talking is no cure; neither is writing, despite what the poets say. This disclosure provides no special insight, only a few planks of wood over sinking sand. Thus, it is only to those curious about the facts of a writer's life and the serendipitous nature of the act itself that I should mention in passing that this manuscript was originally composed by hand and in the German during the time of my sickness and the months after. For some time, the manuscript had gone missing— accidentally disposed of or perhaps purloined, I thought—until one day I found it concealed behind the lining in my suitcase. Upon rereading it for the first time in many months, I became suspicious that parts of it had been altered and some portions entirely changed. I wondered indeed if I had even written it. Translators often remark that the intimacy in carrying a writer's words from one language to another is a communion unlike any other. And so I began translating the manuscript into the English until it was complete, and then out of competition with myself now or whoever I was then when I had conceived those words, I burnt the original.

—T.H., Winter 2012

Recollection

מ — I remember when I touched my sleeping mother's hair, it sparked in my hands and I thought she was inhuman, but I was young, and only years later would I understand she was under the spell of an erotic dream — I remember a white door emboldened with a laurel wreath leading into a basement where we retreated frequently in the tornado season — I remember how day after day would pass while nothing happened and how, without mercy, time would gather weight, accrete a green patina on the locket I chipped with a long fingernail — I remember the swaying firs made a whanging of rusted girders I thought would collapse — I remember sitting at my desk before my most precious things, sheets of graph paper, diagrams, folders, waterlogged and moulded charts, and then unannounced he would come to me, moving my hand automatically across these pages — I remember the gathering darkness of a thousand incidents I never witnessed, and yet bird by bird they separated themselves into moments of bright singularity — I remember that I possess no true memory of my mother and only know at all she even existed by evidence of my own pale skin and the double helix twisted under it into an X — I remember blurry light, rain on an awning, and then being lifted and placed into a red wagon — I remember when the earth was for me, for the last time in its history, still elastic as cartilage, had not fully solidified into the obstacle of the known, the terrible, stubborn thing called *fact* — I remember *it was the hibiscus winter,* because she said so — I remember writing these words, but only barely, but one after another stonelike in their materiality they are undeniable — I remember remembering a dream, under a low ceiling of illuminated clouds swirling in a tarantella, I rode weeping along the boulevard of an empty city newly in ruins where each crumbling museum was my hidden and sumptuous destitution — I remember someone informed me he had once hanged himself from his swing set, then the memory infected me, became my own — I remember a small, A-frame house, and watching the hawthorn wasting in an emollient sea wind — I remember a white door — I remember it was the hibiscus winter — I remember thinking I had been comatose a thousand years, though this is surely false, and in my uncorroborated absence the whole fungible world in a moment of chemical agony had changed in irreversible ways — I remember how everything tasted dark — I remember things I've never felt (a seagull feather brushing my lips, a turquoise shell, my shoulders festooned with flowers) — I remember thinking what was in my mind was put there by others, by books

I read, by objects I looked at but did not own — I remember wondering if other memories remained in the twilight regions of my mind where my failed loves were soil, and if soon someone would enlighten me to things I had done and then, years later, I would remember them as real — I remember tender hands covered in snow — I remember the city, the flames immanent as flowers, patient to burst forth — I remember my favourite word once was —

Oslo, Winter 2011

₪   My writing is the offspring of a suborned father
without a country and a profane void of a mother
whose sadness was without referent. From their
fleeting encounter, a chance assignation, everything
I have penned was conceived, and within the pass-
ing of a cloud, orphaned. Consider this "fact": a man
and a woman — called X and Y, respectively — both
displaced, both wild-eyed and exiled, in both wan-
derlust was evoked by the rustling of a flag and the
geometric cross-stitching of bridge cables through
which wet wind beckoned in the moonlight as he
gripped the back of her neck. Northeast and north-
west, they branched to separate truths, where what
awaited them they were unsure. You've seen this scene
before, narrowed by your window. There: a decrepit
schooner half sunk in dark and the mechanical whir
of a cicada somewhere was turning to ice. The para-
dox of sky: a door and a graveyard. The woman mak-
ing the sign of an X for her heart. The man making
the sign of a Y for his heart. Dearly beloved. Dearly
departed. Which way the wind blows? Consider this
"fact": early on I was taught language was schizoid,
one half reserved for the things of this world and half
for the brutal rush of time for which the things of this
world were moments time accreted into a density we
could feel, like the rough cut of a brick, and through

laughter or weeping understand it was a memory we held onto and whether true or feigned, mattered less than possession. As an infant, I was possessed by language, would wake nights with it fermenting in my mouth, incomprehensible words and dreams which, though I was helpless to write down, I knew even then would be an autobiography of fever. Unblinking, I would count backward from zero into an imaginary and negative realm of decreasing absolute magnitude where I hoped I might discover a pinprick, a small eye-tear in the fabric into which I could slip a gaunt arm. The melodrama inside me eroded into a sorrow I would learn to pick apart and reassemble the way my mother Y (if she existed) may have, in a huddled alley, pulled a bone from a fire. She emerges where two irreducible thoughts — genetics and desire — collide. Consider this "fact": though there is no way to prove it and the effort to could only lead to suicide or worse, here at the end of the twelfth month with no mark of another soul approaching down the long and meandering road, overgrown with brush and fallen trees that leads to the A-frame, I have begun to suspect I am the final iteration of a degraded sign whose meaning will extinguish with me. This prospect has accrued the status of an unconfirmed, but incontrovertible truth. One could even say I have become inspired by the idea. Each word laid end to end would lead to this conclusion. Wait and see. Into my journal I have poured an antique fascination with provenance and ownership equal to a collector of Russian nesting dolls, one haunted by the memory of the other, smaller and smaller. The smallest holding a thimble-breath of air, just enough for the word *reproduction*. Dear Reader, I believe I have encountered you in a dream, mine or yours dimly remembered, and saw — reflected in the mirror you beamed as a signal across the years — my own surface and in that depthless instant recognized how we were together, and how nothing mattered as long as through a fungal season of rain and pink shadow we were with each other. Have you not brooded so, your dark body turning to salt as the supple wind moved like a logarithm through the leaves and in the distance the tall melted buildings were a secular colour? Consider this "fact": walking separately my mother and father were the circumference of a diaspora spreading over the globe like a cobweb. I was already in her womb, a lightbulb under a taut shade. I was forming as a complex archipelago of ideas. A convexed life washed over my unborn eyes as I watched out and later thought in the accumulating iron silence of days I would compensate for all the distortions and for all the erased scenery with a thousand reversed birds aloft over the receding, receding world.

Berlin, Winter 2009

ⅎ   The grace of waking is the sleep that follows. The grace of waking is the sleep that follows. The grace of sleep is the wake that follows. The grace that follows. The phrase looped over and over as I lay awake and asleep the film reel of snowy mountains shuttled past my eyes in the dark feeling. Over and down. Whether early into the night or late toward morning, whether the day had already passed, had turned with a half-twist clockwise or counter like a Möbius strip and begun anew to repeat itself I could not tell, nor would it have mattered, for time blurred and yet at that point in my life, during those incremental years which felt like a railroad being built at a snail's pace toward some unknown city, it seemed there was no progress, as if I were always floating between the reality of my mattress and the play of light and shadow whether my eyes were opened or closed. I remember sensing one moment that if I craned my head out the frost-speckled window I might have seen the name of the last station in stencilled letters, perhaps an antique font, and an older man boarding at the last moment a train in the other direction. And if I waited a few more moments and rose up out of my berth, opened the window, and looked ahead might I have seen the name of the same station approaching through the drifts, then the echoing chamber of its Second

Empire glassy morning and iron and the same man exiting the train in the other direction stare up at me with a look of recognition? And I remember thinking as I pulled the white sheet up over my eyes as I had as a child and then opened them, I would have seen the intermittent sun from the snow-covered firs and the dark columns of electricity poles spaced every half kilometre wash over the sheet and leave their mark on my eyes like a palimpsest after I closed them and saw myself with luggage in one hand and the other steadied on shoulders of those seated as I walked backward down the aisle, feeling nauseated, as the train to Berlin shunted forward with its awful momentum against each step that brought me closer to the little cabin where I would slip into my bunk and pull the sheet up to my chin and lie there with my eyes open for how long I would not know because sleep would come, as it always did for me, with a rush of amnesia. I believe I have been subject throughout my life to bouts of fainting, sudden collapses in energy that have left me bereft and have found me waking after a spell of narcolepsy in an empty theatre, or on the shag carpeting in a rundown boardinghouse in Zurich, or on the way up the stairs or down, I forget, in a rented apartment, perhaps near Cologne where I know I once visited, resting for a second with my hand on the rail until a brief tap on the back and a *hello* by a stranger returned me for a while to this world and with it to the haunting awareness that I was unwell. When I would come to, it was as if I had answered a telephone in the dark, startled and flummoxed by a voice of someone calling through the tunnels of sleep and my first reaction was a dazed, meaningless word, empty of content, something to indicate not more than I was there: *Speaking,* I would mutter. And as I would rest upright in my bed recounting what had happened or what had not while I was away, wherever it was that I went when I slept, trying to remember whether on one particular trip I had kept walking through the square in search of calm in the high-ceiling interior of a nearly empty café or rather I had first paused some distance and stared at a young, uncommonly pretty girl listening through a small portable radio about the size of a book to Edith Piaf's "Les Mots d'Amour" while erasing something in her journal before I restarted my search for the café where I would take a table in the shade, out of sight from others, and there begin to think of her. And as I later lay in bed struggling to recall this or other memories, the scenes would exfoliate before my eyes, peeling away to a caustic whiteness of theatre screens and leaving me with the impression that perhaps each moment had been imagined, the red cobblestones through which a few blades of grass had grown and the feeling of dyspepsia at the realization that the other tall, thin, long-armed girls with high cheekbones cooling by the Mannerist fountain were likely Romanian prostitutes. Or was the etiology of this feeling not that they were, but that I wanted them to be, that I would have it no other way and this possibility left me feeling I had betrayed myself and that perhaps I had become an unreliable narrator in my own novel driven by undisclosed impulses I sublimated into writing. *But this isn't a novel,* I remember telling myself, as I wrote the words on my palm for good measure, *it's my life,* and yet I sometimes would wonder then and still now if the person who is writing and the person who is being written about are of the same mind, are on the same proverbial page. From the earliest days memory would come in black and white sequences often visually layered with films I had watched over and over until they began to deteriorate, sometimes right in the middle of watching or in the midst of a dream my father's face — how I pictured he would appear — would superimpose over Charles Foster Kane's or over the faceless Peter Lorre in *M* purchasing a balloon when the projector's heat would eat through the emulsion and I would wake up in a beam of sunlight as if I too were simply a projection of some superior intellect and then collapse wetly back into the mattress. The grace of waking is the sleep that follows, I would whisper into my own ear, falling asleep before the last word hit the air, my mouth parted like a fish. I waited to be resuscitated even as I envisioned someone would slip into my room and next to the clock-radio drop a DNR order, and once and forever I would follow the staircase out to the street to the station where, with her hair strangely piled up in the shape of a conch shell, a woman, perhaps my mother, who looked like Edith Piaf, was waiting for my departure. I was and still am homeless in the dark, and thus liberated. And whether sleep was for a few minutes of refuge or for hours that would slide into whole days filled with wide blank fields where sunbeams formed shifting geometries of line and angle, at some moment inevitably I would find myself, I was always finding myself in those years, gripping a suitcase as the hydraulic door suctioned its breath behind me and the train trundled into the mountain like a centipede. I would watch the wind speed along the sides of the illuminated cellular windows, sixty per second past rain-filled quarries, small German farms of thatched cottages set back from the rails, and the white fluorescence of cobra lights through which drifted snow, each flake's hexagonal symmetry visible, and I knew — and such was the probable source of my unease — the unblinking train's eye created out of the ether the screeching space in front of it. My lungs rising and falling. Each trompe l'oeil was where desire, whether real or celluloid, would in a moment of lucidity materialize and disappear and if I were in an instant summoned to the triangular door of the A-frame where I live and write, I would be as apt to see a funnel cloud forming on the horizon as I would Oslo with its leaning cluster awash in borealis light, so green I would wonder if it were the glasses I wore. For reasons unknown to me, I was certain my life was moving to a predetermined end and I wondered then and now if I had arrived at that end or if I had somehow passed it and was now to live out my remaining years retrospectively. Both thoughts filled my stomach with ice water, an endless melancholy in the context of flux, and all I could do was hope that the next turn would be beautiful rather than worse.

Berlin, Winter 2009

ℼ You cannot judge a man for what comes auto-
matic to him, but you can rest assured that later, years
after you leave, he will judge himself, and once the
judging starts, it will never end: it too will be auto-
matic. So it has been of that period in my thirties
when I took to the habit of frequenting the brothels
clustered in the old Art Nouveau commercial district
of Berlin where the women and girls, mostly Persian
and Eastern European, would serve me tea in a tulip-
shaped cup. For reasons inexplicable, my thoughts
had become increasingly distracted and disturbed by
the slightest sensation as I grew older, and I would
find myself repeatedly in these quarters when the
weather turned cold and the cobblestones were slick
with a mixture of rain and oil that created rivulets of
colour that recalled spotted koi I had once seen in a
Japanese reflecting pond surfacing as if to kiss the air.
As I remember it now, I would arrive at their draped
windows, often forgetting why it was I had come
and sometimes just as I laid my finger to the door-
bell I would recall, as if the sound had bounced the
memory back to me, I had left with the intention to
purchase some eggs and a newspaper around the cor-
ner. Or sometimes I would stand discombobulated,
suspecting some stranger — perhaps a hungry child
or a mail carrier with a package under his arms —

had rung my door. And then water tapping my shoes, the curtain pulled aside by an elegant hand with red nails, my gyroscopic brain would regain its momentary orientation and balance and I would proceed into a perfumed world of muted voices. The books and paintings I had studied through the years led me to imagine these interior rooms were filled with Pre-Raphaelite consumptives lounging beneath blue lampshades of long flowing tassels that reminded me of jellyfish floating up through the dark sea borne aloft on their own interior luminescence that divers everywhere associate with poison. And no matter how many times the image was dispelled, it would return as I walked down the narrow hallway as its six doors fell closed in succession like a row of dominoes. I turn to this subject now, because I recall how for my thirty-third birthday I sat in an alfresco café in Charlottenburg that had once been a planetarium bombed during the war. The seats still encircled the rusted insectlike projector perched on spindly legs in the centre as if sending invisible beams of Orion and the Great Bear that I contemplated on the cracked, eggshell dome above the tuxedoed waiters when a woman's calling card mysteriously dropped from the sky like a piece of wartime propaganda and landed on the fish skeleton stretched across my plate. I plucked it just as the server, as if protecting me, I later thought, snatched the dish with a gloved hand. I recall the card's tawdry insignia of a fanged serpent coiled around a heart-shaped apple was one as a nine-year-old boy in the orphanage I had spotted in a street parade decorating one side of a fighter plane's nosecone, the other, a buxom girl in white shorts on a swing whom I stared at as I scampered along the perimeter of the silent crowd. Back then, the twin images had seized my attention because the night before I had woken from a reverie in which I was trailing a shirtless old man walking along a road abutted with abandoned four-story apartment buildings, formerly proud emblems of the bourgeoisie, now eaten away by years of sniper fire. Riddled with holes, the buildings loomed like huge termite mounds, unpainted, the walls dun and dust, whorls of wind reverberating in their empty casements and colonnaded verandas where women — mothers and daughters — once stood in colourful dresses to survey the world as they gradually dissolved into nothingness. As the wind began to blow a little harder from the east, the air was so dense with particulate matter that to see in my dream I was obliged to close my lids and run my young fingertips in the ruts on the colonial wall that seemed to go on forever. The body of the dreamer is paralyzed by a chemical the brain releases, though in the somnambulist it is missing, so his imagination is free to wander. I have often felt this condition has seized me even in my waking state, my eyes filled with the fogged-over look one sees in others filing out of a theatre in a single stream under a marquee of yellow bulbs befitting another era, and into the sudden overexposed light of midday. The mere recrudescence of a sign is no reason to ascribe it meaning and the recurrence of patterns of behaviour is, I feel, thoroughly arbitrary in most instances. Even my memories are not repetitions so much as reenactments forming new clusters at each moment of recall. The chamber music, I remember, was barely audible above the chirping yellow parakeet neurotically scratching the bars of its elaborate Victorian birdcage, which seemed a replica of the Palm House in the Royal Botanic Garden. While this rather attractive courtesan in furs — I will call her Ms. M. — with her hair behind her ear like a ribbon of light began to politely enquire what my name was, why I was there, what my tastes were, if I were single, I peered around the room, noting its small details knowing someday they would come back to me: a Chinese vase with a blue floral and dragon glaze, a map of East Germany in a state of advanced deterioration, and a black-and-white security monitor on a bookshelf filled with VHS tapes whose labels I was straining to decipher when I began to bleed rather heavily and for a sustained period from both nostrils.

Berlin, Winter 2009

₪   Though it was immediately clear to anyone who met me, it took me years to realize that at seemingly random moments of my life, I fell into periods of near delirium, during which I would lose consciousness of time. If I happened to be reading, as was often the case, I would place the book facedown in the grass and with a dim and glazed look take to walking in a waking dream through the winding streets of the city through the night and into the earliest hours as newspapers and pastries are delivered to the cafés and merchants cleaning sidewalks with their hoses would glance quizzically, curious about the motives of a solitary wanderer at sunrise. Sometimes in the grip of a somnambulistic episode, I had been known to begin speaking in a language other than my mother tongue, one I had never trained in or had only the most passing familiarity with, such as the few words one learns in another country where one's time is deemed in advance a layover, no matter the duration. I had been known to ask the day of the week in broken Mandarin to a puzzled teenager at a kiosk in New York selling theatre tickets or to return in the middle of the night to the front desk at a hotel where I happened to be staying in Germany and enquire in Arabic why the flowered carpet in my room was dark green. Subsequently, doctors diagnosed me with multiple sleep disorders — confusional arousals, bruxism, periodic limb movement, and forms of automatism, including writing while slumped at my desk like the artist in Goya's etching, though the sleep of reason has produced no monsters, only letters and disquisitions on miscellanea: the marriage customs of countries I never visited and some wholly invented, on the conical symmetry of seashells (a subject I know nothing about, though I have a faint memory of my mother as a meticulous collector), and on at least one occasion, an attempt to capture the night when Verlaine in London slapped Rimbaud, his "exquisite creature," with a fish round the face and fled to Belgium threatening suicide as he left, but the writing broke off. The humiliation in the younger poet's bewildered eyes must have woken me. And upon waking my writing bore little in the way of logic and its looping and attenuated sentences swirled across the page like a butterfly with a damaged wing, a child's scribblings from the wilder shores of love. Suffering from a recurrence of acute parasomnia, I once rose out of the confines of my bed in a trance, and rather than depart alone, fastened the leash to the harness of my dog, who undoubtedly perplexed at being roused hours after midnight nevertheless made his way down the wooden stairs, my hand skimming the wax banister to a curtain lit from behind by a streetlamp, guiding me as he would a blind man across the cobblestones, the cord a nerve channelling unspoken, inchoate thoughts and impulses from my mind to his. On this occasion, I was led out to the desolation past the railroad tracks and the industrial canals where in my normal state I would travel in the future to have a key duplicated or a chair reupholstered by a woman from Greece named Ms. V. whose specialty was sewing patterns as elaborate as the underside of a starfish, and I woke briefly, startled by a car horn, I thought, or the siren of an ambulance two blocks over, or perhaps because a crane lifting into the air an empty BSL shipping container that was to be converted into modular housing for an artist commune momentarily cast a shadow over the street, but soon enough I slipped back under and was led an additional kilometre west to the Brutalist concrete high-rises that since the 1960s marked a sudden and definite threshold rarely crossed from either side. The water- and rust-stained edifices, fourteen in total, seemed to attract musty weather, for the southern walls of each were enveloped in a carpet of moss and nearly every third window by my count held a flag from Algeria or Morocco to repel the glare at noon and conceal the sense at night that life within possessed the eerie claustrophobia of an aquarium. These images slid on the aqueous humour of my eyes like drops of oil, leaving a thin film through which to see the imaginary world in all of its drowsy wind by which I remembered it, in particular a man in this eighties leaning over a railing with an outstretched hand that appeared to gesture at some ominous force approaching behind, but when I turned and looked back at him, there was just a rustle of curtains. No one on either side of me. The chance for recognition, for empathy, or even simple contact was lost. Your placid surface betrays nothing of the debilitating guilt you harbour unaware; like a ventriloquist's doll you speak without understanding the words, or even their source; sometimes I wonder you weren't born, but merely "uttered," Dr. T. R. said to me, a psychiatrist with whom I carried on a brief affair until the transference was too much. This was her reply after I concluded relaying my story. I kept silent on the irony of her claim, for she herself seemed no more than a medium to me, our sessions in the lamp-lit dimness of her decrepit living room in Berlin were only séances by another name, and the glow in her eyes was my final confirmation that the theories she had read but which remained divorced from her world appeared to have taken possession of her. I had divulged that I had been raised in a small town dominated by a frightening armoury in the style of a Moorish fortress with reinforced clinker bricks, narrow lancet windows that were always dark, and four octagonal towers where the last guard stood fifty years ago though I was sure inside was a record of brutal acts perpetrated in the basement shooting range and Roman baths. Its impenetrable emptiness drew from me the worst of my coiled imagination. As a boy, I would routinely walk twenty minutes out of my way to avoid it, circumambulating the dark structure, which cast a pall over the district, absorbing all of the light around it, and even now when I am fully awake listening to a news program on the radio the condemned building is never far from my mind, which fatigues me. There is no pleasure in learning it has been razed to the ground. The thought wakes me at night. I have learnt to cope with my sleep disorder by tying a ribbon around a wrist to the headboard at night, but often I outwit myself, become loose from the entanglements meant to protect me. *After a half-century of hard work and reflection, the wall is still there. Nature—or rather, my nature—remains mysterious,* Matisse, the accused orientalist, wrote. Increasingly I have come to believe what others with greater insight and a stomach for the truth know at a younger age and learn to accept with bemused resignation: that life is no more than a series of linked encounters, like beads on a string, one thing following another in a sentence through time, in a sentence that is the flow of time. Every writer is a man or woman resuscitated, brought back for a little while before being dismissed. While I was hovering in bed barely asleep, my father would sneak in to check on me. Sometimes he came in the shape of a stranger, but his black eyes with a mark of sorrow never changed. When I was younger I could run so fast my shadow would fly off me. I would leave it behind in the city where I was born. There was no city, only my mother's arms. Dear grief, hermetic as a goat's skull. The future where you are, but how to get there except by waiting another year.

New York City (lyric)

₪   There's nothing latent in my wireless imagination where everything, even the heart's muscle, is public. Give me one more love song and I'll destroy it. Orpheus looked over his shoulder because he wanted Lili Brik to disappear, the only way to save himself for the poems he thought he'd write before thirty-six arrived, a shock in its chamber. Oh mother. Oh love. Beauty enters wrapped in furs and the whole train to Moscow suddenly unsure of itself, the revolution suspended between wheels: "Down with Symbolism. Long live the living rose!" The moment the chimp recognized he was human, he began to paint over the mirror. These days, mystery floating in the recesses of the plaza, a memory of green sky high above us like glamour and the history surrounding us forgotten for a minute, then we're cold. Every woman begins as a description. A brochure. A leaflet. Love made into origami. This one's now for July. This one's now for August. This one's now in the wave pool, buoyed by the chlorine and sense of possibility, as if the water were in me and churning and could this feeling last forever and that seagull, you don't have to think. Sometimes you have to be shot in the heart in order to stop dreaming. These days of false humour and sequins, like Jean Nouvel's windows, we look in from the outside because we're fortunate to be poor and part of the city. Every city begins as an accident and soon becomes a need. The player-piano melancholy through the avenues now that the night is quiet ushered in by a line of crows as if pulling a photographer's cloth. Finely granulated static after the daily life counting coins in our solitude after the dry cleaners after the loneliness of the mall at closing, the lights in the fountain turned off, after that you were, after the ornamental civic gardens after the letters tossed from a balcony after the street that ended at a power plant and a river you never drank from, you were, then the orphanage then the House of Assignation then the locked door then the brain scan, you were, the nonfunctional façade after the mattress store after the Museum of Mind Over Matter after that after all that, you were, and the great throbbing crowd once in super slow-mo formed a Rorschach blot, the visuals moving to the melody of a soundtrack, I don't have a map, she said, I just enter the territory — *I love you to this point.* A leaf. A few thoughts on paper. Nature doesn't grow on trees, the critic said, but we don't believe her because we don't believe in Nature, and even her dress is synthetic and her glasses have no lenses so how can she see the moon, or the flag planted there for Marilyn? These days, the intricate architecture of our past lives, the rhythm and beauty

of it, the way you could walk into a stanza at midnight
and surprised to find me at the desk, our home, it was
an idea I grew inside of, and if asked to describe these
days, what I would say would fail, as does every poem
at the title. I'm remembering in Berlin remembering
you and I'm remembering in New York remembering
you and I'm on a bus by Tupper Lake remembering
you for the first time I can't, the morning in blades of
light through the pine trees, a kind of triage. Every
map begins as a legend and ends with a woman on
the Bosphorus where the blue is so supple you wore
it as a scarf and then you took a shuttle called a meta-
phor. In forty years, I'll be dead if I'm lucky. These
days, three o'clock in the afternoon of November, the
Eiffel Tower a radio transmitter of secret signals to
the befuddlement of the professor who thought life
was fixed in amber and that one's home could never
turn into a pawn shop or that no one would blow up
the Louvre and replace it with a W, rather than these
love letters to the people of Juarez. We walk through
the streets like a seam in Barthes's stocking, we're
where the threads come together before they unravel.
All that's solid melts into money and the day ends
with a comma, and even belatedness is marketed like
the colour green will wash the dirt out of your mouth
and with it another philosophy of progress. The city

in which you left me I give it back like remorse. My
breath in your deaf ears, we're both bodies, only yours
in autumn is gone.

Recollection

רו — I remember a strange family had taken me into its arms, welcoming me "home," a lost and important part of their life's dream, they claimed, and when I heard those words instantly I developed fever — I remember red velvet wallpaper shaped with concentric circles which when focused upon seemed to spiral and thought this is a sign of my volition, my ability to move things, and this, I remember thinking, would grow stronger in the coming years I feared — I remember as a young boy wanting someone to take me inside from the wind — I remember on Ms. M.'s dress an embroidered map of Europe before the war where desire shared a border with Russia — I remember how I dared to cross my heart in secret when I was sure no one was looking — I remember the parakeet would fly away over the fields for weeks at a time, leaving me to my own thoughts, and then would return suddenly at night with new words that left me transfixed — I remember how vexed I was on the eve of our departure into the city — I remember kneeling on the floor, sucking at a cut on her fingertip — I remember the description of the bright interior archive was torn, the understory would remain unspoken — I remember the poets year after year praising the amaryllis — I remember red was the colour of circle, red was the colour of being looked at

— I remember becoming entranced, my words began to dissolve with each repetition, each involuntary arm movement when I peered up the branches of the bare autumn and when I turned away — I remember at four being called an interruption — I remember the helicopter hovering, pivoting over the skyscraper in strong weather, someone unseen pulling up the rope ladder — I remember they put a tag with my name on it about my neck — I remember how she made me feel urgent and in the heart of the plaza — I remember something pregnant in me — I remember one day I began to suspect I was a minor character in my own story after years of believing I was in the lead — I remember how I didn't want to be myself for a while or be by myself, for being me was lonely even when I pretended to be someone else — The last thing I remember was promising myself — A scrap of tinfoil placed in my mouth and I thought for a moment how it was like —

Oslo, Winter 2011

ℝ   With my awakening, there was a buzzing in my
left ear — the static sound of an itch — as if a code
in a last desperate measure were being whispered. A
secret I suspected I was meant to die with. The mag-
nified sun zeroed in my eyes. Sat up, shaking my head
no, no. My mind a miasma of thoughts. In the eaves
hung silence and a single light bulb at the end of a
knotted cord swayed slightly. The A-frame quavered
in thunderstorms and the day would come when it
would tumble into the sea. I envisioned it many times
when staring from under my umbrella in the garden
amongst the lightning strikes and lilies. Through the
alcove window, beyond the decaying walls of this
small, desolate estate, I saw the bright smoke stack
of the incinerator on the hill, which fumed night and
day without end from the moment I can remember
first laying my eyes upon it and saying the word *incin-
erator,* emit a blast of saffron fire straight into heaven
and then, to my wonder, it ceased. A fly on the win-
dowpane shook its wings, rubbed together tiny hairs
on its front legs in irritation. I did not know and did
not want to know how long I had been asleep, but
I suspect it was longer than I could imagine, longer
than I could have ever dreamt. I lay nude, washed
ashore in a tempest of rain and leaves, regurgitated
back into the world for another go-around. I had

been at the tail end of a dream that came frequently in different forms to me for the past year but whose meaning loitered faintly on the edge of my apprehension. It was a dream that seemed to trail me through my waking life, yet hanging back like a small child, as if it had something it were afraid to tell me. I suspect the dream has been dormant in my brain from my earliest days when I was found riding in a red wagon pulled through the streets by a sheepdog. The woman who would soon assume the role of my mother lifted me up into the air, held me against the sky, and said simply *Ahhhh*. Though my analyst, Dr. T. R., called this a lie, I remember the moment precisely, for it was the first time I had seen the world from what seemed to me then a great height and the sense of awe that emerged out of my wordless mouth was equal to that of my new mother's. For a year now, I have had dreams of this memory and of other memories I can no longer recall and dreams of memories of a city of minarets I seem never to have visited and of people whom I seem never to have met, though I am sure these are real memories and not the fabrications of my imagination. For a year now my waking life has itself assumed the quality of a lonely dream. In the sanctuary of sleep I have made my cathedrals. When I close my eyes, those I once knew, whose faces are erased more each receding day, fly to me for a little while in companionship and in terror. Before I woke that afternoon, an aged man in a white frock was bent over me, wearing a cap with a spotlight and about his ears a stethoscope like a pair of deflated horns. He wore a squinted expression of sad curiosity, as if I were a son he never knew and now found too late he fathered one night in an alley with a whore under a trellis of moonlight and afterwards wept, as the moon climbed higher into the sky. This is how it would be: my real mother, the woman of debauched flowers. My fictional mother, a suffocating nurse and a dreamer. Like a priest, father crying downward to death, upward to ecstasy and death, death from above, the whole world sin sin sin. He stared at me with his white eye, pressed the stethoscope against my heart and wept, as if listening intently to an old radio program from the war. In his face I could see planes soaring above London in holy flames as he penetrated her amongst the garbage and wharf rats. The entire time he stood over me, I knew I was in a dream, but his sorrow was real and to comfort him, I summoned grief home to my heart, but it was gone, both grief and my heart replaced by reports of a world besieged, and as I searched I could not even find the word *sorry*. And the word *sorrow*, well, that is another story. He daubed his worried forehead for a moment with a handkerchief monogrammed *H.E.I.,* paused. A perfect world is right around the corner, and far, far away. Mother, your hair of attic and old coat comes to me on a breeze. The room burnt rose. The red letters of a monogram descending, a branding iron. It was winter, the whole Christian earth buried in a graveyard of snow that fell and fell. A deer with eyes dark as plums looked in through the window. My father began to intone my name in a solemn tongue but it sounded dubbed, as though when he mouthed my name another word emerged. Our shadows stretched, grew larger on the wall. Then in sudden pain, his mouth scrapping mine, there poured from him in a whoosh a storm of fireflies, a golden rain lighting the room in an immolation of tiny loves. He slumped against me and onto his back, a cyclops. Through a lambent hole in the dark, a ray of a film projector on the ceiling. And then, on a grainy Super 8 reel, I saw myself, as I had so many times before, an infant crawling on all fours through long grass following my mother's yellow hair slipping through a crack in the murk, luminous with pinpricks of light and the falling leaves of a dead autumn that would cover her and these words if I failed to save them.

Oslo, Winter 2011

ॻ   Possession is nine tenths of a mother. I began
to suspect this even then in those early years when I
was the one boy in the Asylum for Lost Children who
could not sleep. It was postulated that my mother had
been in typical fashion "seduced and abandoned"
as a young woman and laboured in a neo-Victorian
brothel but one town away from the narrow bed
where, after being passed like a pail of water through
a sequence of hands at a house fire, I had finally come
to rest. I would lie there awake on my twin mattress
waiting in a state of suspended animation, as if about
to be x-rayed, and when the nuns on their rounds
leaned over in the dark I could detect an odour of fer-
mentation under their curls and was sure they were
to my ill-begotten mind from another world. An odd
assortment of groans and hums reverberated through
the shuttered rooms, as if a pipe organ had been sub-
merged underwater, and I would in the depths of my
insomniatic childhood when sleep was nowhere in
sight, through the sheer force of will teleport myself
to what I later learned was the primal scene of trauma,
the child's witness to the violence visited upon the
mother by the father's crumpling intercourse and
once there I would begin dreaming. For obvious rea-
sons, this moment of coupling was impossible for me
to observe, but I feel I have not been immune from

its effects, and when as an adult, perhaps it was out of compensation as much as interest that I read of Little Hans's cautionary tale, the toddler cocooned in a doublet and lederhosen standing in the muted door watching in horrified wonder what would one day morph before the eyes of Freud into a fear of horses. The scene I confess was the wrong one but a lure nevertheless, for my mother at the instant of my conception was, I sensed, actually alone, sitting at her escritoire in a robe, like a mildly dishevelled stage actress, a vulcanite hair comb holding a small spray of asters above her ear, and in her hand an oyster-shell pen perched over a letter as she waited for the proper word to form in the drop at the nib. Orange hydrangeas in the halogen light of a gathering dusk. I think two thoughts at once and the impossibility of expressing them as one is where anxiety and later eros originate. My mother was, I am certain, always like this: on the precipice of writing, and yet waiting for a knock on the door, perhaps for once a suitor with roses to announce himself and mercifully interrupt her. She must have those many months later when the disturbances inside her marked an unavoidable tran-sition, turned to the complexly brocaded wallpaper and upholstery that darkened her room and looked in speculation and pain when my legs breached from her like a wish: the letter Y. This peculiar detail has never been adequately explained to me though I have poured for hours over the few anonymous letters I received through the years — matted to my left heel was a small, partially decayed leaf and under my newborn fingernails the slightest evidence of soil. I was pulled backward into the world, a sensation that still grips me when I sleep, as if drawn by some inhuman, magnetic force down the mattress toward what I do not know. At some point the past and the present departed — *Dearly beloved, we are gathered here today. . . .* The slow blotting of faces and words. If you could dream another time, then perhaps you could live in it, the voice in my head, which I facetiously called the Narrator, said to me. I did not know then nor now who or what to trust because the thoughts in my head often seemed unoriginal and would enter without permission, where once implanted formed colonies of association the way bacteria assemble and mutate. By the time I was approximately twenty, my memory of my childhood was thoroughly corrupted as to be quite useless, and yet the little I remember of my earliest days in the Asylum remains remarkably clear as a delicate insect perfectly preserved in amber. I recall a sheepdog as tall as my shoulder that took a liking to me for some reason and we would walk together among the elderberry bushes as another dog unseen to us walked barking occasionally along the outside of the stone wall. I like to think the dog was from the neighbouring houses whose weather-stained wooden roofs I could glimpse from the top step, barely making out the mushroom satellite dishes that sprouted under the wet sky. I like to think now if I were to rest in a field of rococo grasses, pollen and dandelion seeds of late spring, all this life and allergy . . . that if I were to stay in one place long enough . . . a soft cough from the small crawling things of this world. I like to think when I close my eyes I am able to see Caspar David Friedrich's explorer on a craggy outcropping over the roiling somnolent clouds, with his back turned to his creator (Herr Friedrich himself), captured a second before he leaps. Or perhaps he remains paused in the ghostly fulgent light of his survey, the atmosphere suffused with ripe lilies, soft summer mouldering of leaf and meal, the corpse of a deer biodegrading under a disinterested, camera stare into a rope of purples and cobalt blues as the intricate scarab beetle for whom the universe is death goes about its work. Moon, dark spoor. A thousand decays. Out of a mother's mouth emerges art like a worm, which is also life.

Oslo, Spring 2010

℩ When I was living a short flight from the nearest city in a Mansard house in a state of advanced disrepair but with high attic windows that opened west over a fjord where oyster boats plied the waters at sunrise and sunset, I entered a period of nearly complete isolation in which my withdrawal was such that an entire day would pass without my uttering a word. To forestall the dangers of loneliness, I took to long walks downhill to the coastal tidewaters to inspect the channels cut by glaciers in the last ice age and then would explore the crags for the afternoon, on occasion encountering a nodding fisher or a woman on a cantilevered patio beating a rug with a broom handle, and as I sat on the dock I would recall reading about the wretched conditions under which the port was constructed and wondered how many of the workers who tumbled into the depths where the temperature hovered just above freezing were preserved at the threshold of metabolism within a few metres of each other. The villages in the immediate area were picturesque without exception, but almost uniformly composed around small harbours of simple red barns and unadorned white clapboard houses whose shutters, come the first of October, were drawn one after another on cue. The region spoke a welcomed insularity and few pleasures during the dark winter months, as if life were a matter to be endured, a long sentence one accepted, for in such isolated climes — reachable by boat or seaplane — any other world existed in a realm of fancy where only children and strangers resided. The whole landscape seemed to me then sheltered from time, not unlike the exquisitely detailed glass snow globes that lined my bookshelf, one every Easter wordlessly arriving in the mail in a wooden crate packed with straw and centred like an egg. They were sent from a great uncle I never met but whose whereabouts for several years of my boyhood I could track at some delay on his travels across Europe and to America by marking with a thumbtack on the large map taped to the ceiling over my bed the city or shrine he visited, and though unable as a child to deduce the true purpose for his journeys, I would imagine as I peered into each diorama beneath a ponderous glass one associates with clairvoyants and a base of handcrafted filigreed pewter and silver, which must have doubled the cost, each pilgrimage was for no other reason than to acquire the small treasures he would box and mail without a letter. A train tunnelling through a Christmas storm into the Bavarian Alps. The black Virgin of Montserrat submerged in an underwater grotto. And two figure skaters beneath the trusses of the Eiffel Tower passing each other on the ribbons of an infinity symbol while a tinny piano solo played if the butterfly key was wound. Etched into its lapidary surface was simply the word *Paris*. My great uncle's travels apparently came to a conclusion on a beach in Los Angeles where starfish falling from the sky in a shakeable universe were larger than the young family walking in profile with their terrier. I learned to look upon the world from an insurmountable distance, as if orbiting above or under it as the case may be, attached by a slight tether, which were it to tear would set me adrift backward in space. Writing is a form of travel by which we never arrive. It would take me years to understand that lesson, my cities — London, Berlin, New York — were memories to which I could no longer return, for they belonged to someone else in a grey twill suit worn without a tie and a certain elegant blank stare that betrayed none of the circumstances of its origin. Like a planarian cut in half, I would every few years regenerate into a new version, without wounds, without scars, without history marked on my skin, my heart rebuilding its tissue suture by suture. With the relocation to another city, another apartment in an endless series of spaces temporarily inhabited, a few dress shirts wrapped in the dry cleaner's plastic, a few small paintings arranged on the wall in a makeshift life, the soul moving into a new story. That spring I walked the fjord, the atmosphere smelt of minerals and ever a threat of snow in the uninhabited upper reaches where the carpet of green was uninterrupted by trees. In the middle of the day I once found myself idle under the awning of a silk flower merchant from Iran, running my fingers over the petals and stems of the magnolias, giant calla lilies, anthuriums, philodendrons, so stunned by the quality of their imitation my confused mind worried for a moment they were a patent infringement. On the few occasions when I have been presented with flowers, I have immediately placed them in the light of a window, and proceeded about the daily rituals of boiling water for tea and answering neglected letters, but I always wait in anticipation for the sepals to curl and wilt, to smell their exhaled perfume, and the fallen pollen to dust the sill, noting the day on the calendar, even the hour, at which their vibrancy had begun to putrefy, for it is the peak of their beauty. What a foolish thought. But such was my thinking, as I considered the subtle insult to life of the merchant's flowers, when I startled on the underside of a leaf a dragonfly which flew up into the sun, and my eyes following after for a split second saw through the stained glass of its wings. Once Ms. M. in Berlin in the midst of a blackout stood half-dressed in my white shirt at the desk and ran her fingers across the indented pages of the journal into which I pressed myself and said they felt like Braille. That spring I lay in bed with my eyes rolled back as if to steal a glimpse of my own thoughts as the curtains in my white room blew over me. For months, I could not think. To think would have been to imagine a future. But my future, I was beginning to understand, lay in the past waiting for me to return by railroad, one word at a time. The early painted stars forming a parabola in the sunset's stretched latitude that somewhere looped back into a circuit. I recall how one evening in the fall of 2009 when I was sojourning in Rome, I had crossed a courtyard warm with tomato vines and terracotta and a nurse, just released from work, sat on a bench with *The Sorrows of Young Werther* held high as if advertising the book and murmured a few words to herself as I passed through a beaded curtain into the melody of voices where couples had gathered for a drink, while part of me remained behind, perched over her shoulder like a quotation mark. The two of us, and all the uninvited others who made their appearance and left by a side exit, defined the common space of our listening, the stones settling in the rebuilt campanile, moonlight filtering down like a sonogram over the small enclosed world, a dark flowering.

Copenhagen, Spring 2010

₪   What I do not wish to reveal will be discovered anyway, because I will inevitably tell it by leaving it out of the record. Such is how desire works. So consider this: thirty-five kilometres north of Copenhagen, on a morning of washed-out light that is not uncommon to the region in April, I was following at an ever-increasing distance for the space of an hour a Middle-Eastern woman in her thirties through a field of heather stretching for acres, which were full of grouse that rose up in a great clattering confusion as I waded through, as if I had aroused them from a sleep that had lasted all of their lives. She wore a white dress of muslin and intricate lace resembling a sail wrapped about her shoulders, and unlike myself was able to walk noiselessly through the field without a disturbance, leaving no trail behind her as if her feet were floating through the heather. Glancing once over her shoulder, she lifted her veil, and I saw on her face a sense of wonderment, the way a parachutist looks back before leaping into the ether, then she disappeared over the hillside. By the time I reached the crest she was nowhere to be found on the slow undulations of purple and marbled green ending with a collar of fog on a desolate stretch of seacoast that seemed so cheerless and heartbreaking a place as to be all but uninhabitable. The abandoned lighthouse, plywood in the windows, each with an X on it, conveyed as much. Neither the longer odyssey by which I had arrived at the scrub of dirt and brush and wind-swept trees nor the place I first set sight of her — in a vegetable market or at a petrol station or by a bell tower in a town square — had left any residue by which they might be traced backward, recovered, or recalled without fabrication. But this knowledge by itself would not stop me from trying. Without realizing it I had fallen for some months into the practice of following women through Copenhagen, which lent my otherwise aimless walks a purpose apart from passing time before sleep. It was often the case that I would walk the distance of several blocks, sometimes a kilometre or more into entirely different quarters of the city before I became aware I was, as if on autopilot, keeping pace with a woman threading her way through a crowd, late for lunch, or a business meeting, or, as happened once, back to her apartment building where, catching a door of iron roses right before it closed, I followed and turned into an interior courtyard at the last second, as she ascended the stairs to shower or sleep or talk on the phone or wait for her lover, I had no way of knowing. I rested for an hour, while I stared at the crumbling stones and up at a parcel of sky on a soundless day through which, miraculously enough, a zeppelin glided overhead like a mechanical whale, and I was convinced for a moment it was 1901 again and everyone and everything would be okay for a while. I would never speak to these women — maybe a hundred or more in total — and I would take caution to hang back a few metres to feign a casual coincidence but close enough to breathe a trail of perfume, realizing any recognition would prematurely end the spell I was under and wake me to the ruins of the day. I can only speculate upon what drew me to them other than they walked with an assurance and direction that each step carried them into a future self-determined and entirely their own, while I myself felt each year recede into the past, like a broken ice shelf and on its drift the explorer who having found what he wanted refuses to leave. By the time she would enter an elevator or rendezvous with a companion, which I took as a signal my pursuit was over, I would invariably find myself leaning in a doorway hastily transcribing her height, weight, hair colour, *son habillement,* the shape of her earrings, and then I would invent a name fitting for her, vines scrolling down my pages. Consulting my notebook I can confirm the evening before the woman disappeared through the heather, I had slept in the Inn Bonne Esperance and though I had no appetite despite having not eaten in over thirty hours, had alone taken a dinner of melon, roasted salmon, white tea on a heated patio decorated with holiday lights strung in a few potted begonias, had spoken briefly with the elderly keeper who, so barely animated he seemed to have survived his own death and was now biding his time, proceeded precisely at nine to show me my room. It was strangely adorned with two antique diverging mirrors that were meant to open up the claustrophobic quarters, but which created instead a debilitating sense of disorientation, as if space itself around me were beginning to bend. That night the simplest movements became a trial. Each time I would cross the floor for a glass of water or to retrieve my wallet, multiple versions of myself appeared out of unfathomable recesses in the mirrors, converged in the centre and then dispersed, one turning a corner back into the corridor that now seemed to lead to the basement, two others climbing perpendicular up the walls in different directions, a fourth hanging from the ceiling as I paused. All of this induced a paranoia that I had begun to project onto any surface reflexive of my desire a desire to be seen. I was nauseated, as I always felt when looking at an M.C. Escher lithograph which now I was sure I was in danger of becoming trapped within and so, exiting the room with care, I ventured downstairs to find the owner to request another accommodation, but to judge by all of the open doors he, along with the other two guests, a Jewish couple travelling to Munich, seemed to have departed. It was only later I learnt from reading on the early period of European demonology that convex mirrors were an effective tool for ridding a room prone to unfriendly spirits. It was not a haunting I felt, then or now. Not precisely, unless you can haunt yourself, the former life clawing out of the dead leaves and soil. As I gather my thoughts like the threads of a tapestry, the window I stand in surveys the city's aquamarine office towers populated with accountants, financial analysts, insurance underwriters whose lives, which make ours possible, I cannot begin to imagine, and a few metres below is a cemetery of mature oaks, a storage house enshrouded in such ivy to remove it would cause the roof to cave, and perhaps a hundred tombstones tilted on a slope that steps down to a small river popular with mallards in summer. I know nearly nothing of those buried in the family plots and sepulchres whose eroded inscriptions I can almost read on a clear, dry day with a pair of opera glasses, lives given in battle, victims of cholera, death by isolation, stillbirths, erased suicides. I was once informed graveyards old as this no longer have bodies in them, only names and sun in the branches and an inkling of the future robins bring. Twice a month in late afternoon, two nuns appear, though I never see their arrival, to repair a broken link in the fence, pruning underbrush around the mossy stones with a pair of small scythes, a bit of dirt on the wrist which gets smudged on her forehead and suddenly it is Ash Wednesday, and the sky is unfolding and they have gathered leaves into a wicker basket in the medieval lanes with the dedication of a gardener poised before the fragility of his orchids: *White Moth, Flower of San Sebastian, Mother of Pearl, Apollinaire, Tiger, Hider of the North.*

Copenhagen, Fall 2010

₪   The town where I had passed my childhood was
a favourite subject of my memories about which I
could dwell, even luxuriate, for hours while lying on
a couch alone in a largely empty house bereft of furni-
ture, or while sharing with my analyst, which I often
did with my eyes closed so it seemed to her I was
talking in my sleep and the long monologues that
streamed out of me without any urging as I reclined
on her sofa, imagining it were a raft, flowed from an
underground river whose source, I liked to think,
was the icy meltwater of Norway's Austfonna glacier.
But over years these memories became more infre-
quent and my efforts to conjure them by pouring over
sepia-toned photographs of bridges or schoolrooms
filled at first glance with identical children quiet at
their desks, or by holding in my palm a porcelain
brooch of a young Victorian couple walking horses
beneath two sycamores were to no avail. Then one
day I recognized the transports of my wonder had
left me behind, and the prospect of remaining forever
trapped within the crystal of the here-and-now was
enough to usher in the most severe depression. The
small cache of talismanic objects I had acquired over
time and carefully guarded included, in addition to
the photos and brooches, distressed maps of various
cities in Europe, elaborate corals, pigeon feathers, a

woman's silk ribbon in purple, two miniature masks worn by monkeys during itinerant countryside theatre performances in nineteenth-century China, and a boy's diary with a cross on its cover secured with a tiny rope. Relics of other pasts, they bore no true connexion to my youth. The items were purchased at estate sales and antique stores during the migratory period of my early thirties. I had chosen them out of the disorderly array of possibilities, the sheer randomness of abandoned objects, as evidence for an invented childhood, plot devices if you will, whose fictional quality assumed a truth I could barely deny. I could recall little of my life before the age of puberty and so to compensate for the honeycombed structure of my brain, I took to assembling a glass and teakwood cabinet where at night displayed items were aglow from spectral electricity emanating out of things torn from their context, a quality witnessed in the oddly bright eyes of tropical birds forced to live indoors. Whenever I moved from one apartment to another, from one city to another, as was my wont as soon as a place had exhausted its spell, I would carry the cabinet by hand, a shroud draped over it like the cage of a sleepless parrot, which only served to elicit the curiosity of each passerby on the street. I would install the box on its own stand and immediately rearrange the items by different taxonomies according the usual order — age, size, colour, organic or manufactured by human labour — but also by systems cutting to the heart of the issue with greater quickness — objects that contained sadness, objects that over time would change shape, objects that should not exist, objects that could not be destroyed. But one day the cabinet, which had been built as a portal for my imagination, quite inexplicably metamorphosed into a museum of dead things. The auratic pulsations emitting a diffuse colour that recalled sea glass were simply inert. The suddenness of the change was baffling, but I feared I had robbed them of their special power by handling each with too great a frequency, like the dials of a shortwave radio. To this day, I still feel deep within me a glittering but inaccessible and lost radiance that grows with its distance from my current life, but the use value of this knowledge is as limited as Vermeer's sunlight. That afternoon, I sat in a wing-backed chair facing the cabinet feeling the sun's falling fire on my back, feeling reduced to benumbed speculation, then as the hour reached the mysterious moment when dusk filling the room is exactly balanced by twilight settling over the cobblestoned street, I rose up to walk the eyelid curve of the port in Aker Brygge by the converted shipyards where at night theatre and restaurant patrons departed for the trams as if inside a well-lit belief that could carry them safely beyond the hills. I knew no one within 900 kilometres and as often happens when this terrible realization is visited upon me, I found myself lost in the labyrinth of my own thoughts, watching the small sailboats drifting in the dark harbour like ideas worth admiring. It was then I remembered an elderly man wearing a waistcoat I had once approached on a park bench in London some ten years prior, having just come from Temple Church, where the young choristers draped in their scarlet cassocks had turned into small flames as pollution gathered in the clouds at sunset. In my chiaroscuro'd memory, he looked like Mr. N., the owner of a coop of carrier pigeons from my childhood town. He raised the birds in the attic of his Edwardian mansion as a hobby after his wife had died of inoperable bone cancer because he felt their honing instinct was a perfect metaphor for the human heart. He would drive to the furthest reaches of town, sometimes deep into the Bavarian countryside, always a different route in hopes of confusing the birds to test their fidelity. And then, upon securing an empty scroll to their legs with a ribbon or strands of his own hair if the ribbon had run out, he would release them into the day, only to drive home slowly for he wanted them to wait for him, as if he were the one who had flown away. When I confronted the man to enquire if he were indeed who I thought he was, he replied he had once resided in the same town, but as to being a hobbyist with pigeons, he was clueless what I was speaking about, stating he found the tale odd but charming. Wondering if I myself may not have inadvertently invented the story and not wishing to be dismissed immediately, I asked if he had any recollection of me as a boy from the local orphanage; he said no, but regardless with the wave of his hand invited me to take a seat next to him. The sum of our solitudes, we remained through the evening while the London Eye stared hypnotically from its pupilless centre at the spires of Westminster, at Cleopatra's Needle, at crows floating in air as if nowhere were worth landing, and at us while we sat there unable to move while a line of snow settled in a hushed circle at our feet. That night back in Copenhagen I hailed a car, a warm glow on the taxidriver and from his metre the knowledge that even in stillness time was passing. Out the back window the narrow canyon began to move again, receding into the night like the ending of a melancholy film. A light rain falling. The car gathering speed on an incline never noticed before, a momentum that pushed me gently against the seat and I could not see the driver in the darkness and I wondered if he were still behind the wheel or if it even mattered as water whipped off the windshield in little rivulets into which the people melted, sidewalks awash in colour and then miraculously petal . . . petal . . . petal . . . in a blur. And I was a blur as well, only I could not see I was hurtling through the world.

Copenhagen, Winter 2010

₪   As part of our instruction in the resources of the natural world we were taken without notice to the city aquarium to see the beluga exhibit that was to be crated the next day and transported by boat to America. And I recall as we trekked through the streets in anticipation each of us like dwarves held a long scarf tied at the waist to the Mother Superior marching through the obscure light of morning fog so far in front of us her habit disappeared and those of us near the end of the tether, where I often found myself on our field excursions beyond the orphanage's wrought-iron gates, felt pulled through the clouds swirling about our legs by a horse we could not see. As I write this now, I recall pausing on the street either to stare at a murky scene unfolding in the small, corner park where a cluster of men, including the neighbour Mr. N., wearing vests and houndstooth trousers as if out of a daguerreotype had scattered seeds for pigeons and were now engulfed in a clutter of wings or perhaps I had paused because a memory from my life prior to the orphanage had surfaced and to fully capture the sensation of its return everything inside me came to an abrupt halt. What I do know was that I was pulled so hard by my wrist I fell. The scene was to be the opening sequence of images in a film I very much wanted to direct but am now too old ever to begin, I said to a German woman, Ms. L., almost ten years later in a poorly lit restaurant in Copenhagen in early winter, where I had travelled to visit the gravesite of Kierkegaard, who himself had died from complications of a childhood fall. The woman, I recall, had a barcode tattooed to her wrist and wore two tiny bells as earrings. I said goodbye to her outside as another winter storm gathered in her hair. Despite my protestations, I never saw her again except in the photograph I snapped as we departed and I learnt nothing in Assistens Cemetery except it is a popular spot for young couples seeking isolation. A few moments under dappled shadows before night settles in a water glass. Leave-taking. Silence. I thought of matters of love and death often as a young boy which only made me withdraw further from the small daily rituals of life and as an adult seek out crowds during my travels through Trafalgar Square, Shinjuku, New York where even locals were tourists, everyone in motion. The film stops here. I am recalling this now because the image of the aquarium frozen in time bears almost no resemblance to the sensation of standing in front of it. Eggshell-white, the beluga circling alone in long slow loops through the dark blue water, dissolving into the ink and rematerializing, back and forth as if playing a game of hide and seek, like a ghostly thought one cannot quite capture or a creature from a distant world, its grotesque beak opening and closing behind the soundproof glass, speaking to us in our inaudible childhoods. What I know for certain is if I were to make this film, the woman would not have disappeared in the snow and I would have had her letters arrive at intervals to mark the passage of time for the viewer. She would have written: it is 1999 and I am pale as a watermark. Sombered. To Berlin I've returned to find nothing where I've left it — the café, the opera house, even the colour of the street have changed. And yet from the television tower — a needle through the eye — the city is undeniably there, grimly apportioned out as only we Germans can. She would have written: there is in a narrow lane off Karl-Marx-Allee a used bookstore where the owner has placed in the window a photo of his deceased cat and a Fragonard calendar print of a girl reading and now customers stay away. Nature has formed us, she wrote, nature has formed nothing that does not consume itself, Goethe wrote, she wrote. The little comfort in the ultramarine morning burns off and one's thoughts turn back on themselves like a palindrome. In her next letter, from the summer of 2003: money is a self-organizing infection and left to its own, it replicates uncontrollably. In the next decade, if we get there, the important poetry will be about money. She would have written: I cannot shake the feeling I have been dragooned into a fiction I don't want. At some point, the muse walks through the door, becomes a character in the story and everything changes. At this point, her letters would have ceased, though I suspect she continued to write to me in secret, and so I kept writing to her almost everyday until one morning my letters were returned, bundled and unopened, whereupon I began to read my own words, the latest first and in her voice, like water filling my mind until nightfall. I felt close to her, even as the distance between us grew larger. Then in December I took the train to Berlin determined to find her and instead for reasons not entirely clear, settled into a nineteenth-century farmhouse a local architect had rebuilt into a corrugated box of iron and plate glass. For a season I did little but pace and watch a dervish of leaves outside my window; then, without warning, I returned to Copenhagen.

New York City (lyric)

₪   . . . And how I came to be with you again in the ruins of the Chrysler plant, beneath the coil of silver tubes dangling from the disembowelled ceiling, as if the whole place, what was left unplundered, had been eaten by worms, and the plaster from the mural of workers on the assembly line crumbling like regret when we touched it, and the dreams of Art Deco in which life is elegantly modern and destroys the world in its little way like the Île de France crossing the Atlantic with its passengers tipping oysters as if it were yesterday or 1913 with girls dancing the whirligig and moonlight on the seagulls following the flow of the waste stream. And how I came to be with you again, without warning, when the first notes of a piano recall the aromatics of an oriental lily in a certain hotel in Berlin on Sunday where on a florid but threadbare carpet rested a borzoi with blue eyes so content and utterly still in an enigma all of its own we thought it might have been porcelain. There in the ether stretched through the misfortune of our time zones, and the rows of ones and zeroes where I come to be with you again for a brief moment, relieved, then the screen refreshes its memory and the Skype goes blank and the sky a Mondrian of aeroplanes coordinating a descent into the cantilevered city of glass and a woman sings through my headphones "I am the storm and I am the wonder" and how in the midst of my Swiss illness I came to be with you again in Akihabara, Kreuzberg, on a staircase in Astoria, in Nişantaşı whose malls have x-ray machines to guard the flowering chandeliers of Murano, a burning garden, in the Shilin night market where for a moment I lost you in the rabbit warren of vendors and pushcarts until at the end of the block under a plasma screen selling its own magical lucidity you waited with a rainbow on your face. In the postindustrial quarter the fishbowl cameras film the school of shoppers swimming through the honeyed light of exhaust when an epiphany suddenly happens and reactionary modernism is replaced by Jeff Koons who made it smile and *Chloe in the Afternoon* becomes the Ingres painting it once was, the odalisque with her elongated gaze in a room so warm you could bend the air. And a door slides open to a seacoast of rolling surf crested with fog and a Russian cargo ship piloted by a satellite eases past without a sound, as if someone forgot the volume has been muted, and the silhouettes playing chess in the sand dunes appear in a pantomime as if they too might blow away in the salted wind and welter and whether or not I came to be with you again, catatonic on the grey waters of my mattress wondering equally what soared above in the stars —

radaradaradar — and what swirled below in the illuminated vortex, love and death collapsing into the hole of the other from which each erupted, and how I came to be with you again in the afterlife of sleep I would not remember when I woke, to find myself, as always, locked in the unshakeable present tense of the mako shark. Most certainly a chemical explanation exists for this defect. The woman who rubbed your soul so your life felt electric for once absconds in the middle of a wet snowstorm, steering and staring through the rearview mirror until her guilt is small enough she can no longer care for it. And then just like that she returns in a pair of Louboutins in the Galerie du Passage carrying the very word *desire* into the folds of the theatre curtains, the shutters clicking. In the time it takes for the smashed wine bottle to be recycled into a windshield in Genoa, or for the foreign correspondent to report the body count in Sadr City as a sports score when the roar goes up, or for the bird to become a hybrid that sings for its other half (Khlebnikov's ear perched at the lip of the café table) once the deciphered genome has been rewired and an aria from *Tosca* explodes from a cellphone in a handbag made of python, everything, even our breathing, stops. As it does when the Eurostar slips its head under the Channel and we fall drowsy from excitement. And how I came to be with you again has yet to be determined. The citrine light beyond the minarets and wild quince trees of Tangier are a promise redeemed when the human heart has run out of water or lost its restore point so nothing else works, except goodbye. And now the film is too beautiful we want it to start over before it ends, and in the crushed dark we realize its final flourish has begun. And now the espresso machine is a miniature city and we live on its edges. And how I came to be with you again when remembrance is a species of forgetting. And now the pages of the evening refresh and the man in quadrant four with his back to an alley, is on his way, waving his hand, this early urban winter endured mutely; this is his signature, the same words he won't say transcribed onto the dark sky of his mind, brighter for what they've been through. And now in the hollows of the fertile night every woman is a debased copy of you at your dressing table perfuming your hair as you retrieve a letter from your pocket I had written to you for such an occasion.

Recollection

₪   — I remember a long tracking shot of pale houses (white, red, soft yellow) and a single, grainy tree in each yard unfolding in the slowed-down time of a camera fastened to a white van edging soundlessly along the road — I remember like most children, I came into the world under disgraceful circumstances, the exact details of which I am unsure, are conjecture, supposition, maybe buried in memory — I remember when I learnt of a species of moth that for nourishment sips tears from the eyes of sleeping birds, my first thought was it was too wonderful to be true — I remember thinking the birds only pretended to sleep — I remember lying for minutes beneath the waters of a bathtub as I stared at the distorted stars painted on the ceiling going black — I remember everyday for a year I had no prospects for recovery and would sit in the melting sunlight on a balcony in early spring, the piano of Satie playing in my head and then within a breath was in a café in Mitte where you slowly swirled milk counterclockwise in a cup of tea, a moment added to the history of a day only to forget it tomorrow and by these small accumulated notes: a life — I remember gradually coming to on the metro to discover all other commuters slumped in their seats — I remember what the next bend in the lane revealed hardly seemed real: a small city designed in Helvetica vertically wedged into the cliff at an angle intended to make one nervous — I remember how the images kept unfolding in waves, hurtling forward with an unsustainable velocity, a hawk tumbling through the night air unable to right itself — I remember the day it occurred to me a father's purpose for an abandoned son is perhaps none other than to spark a need for pursuit and an over-investment in the truth origins supposedly disclose — I remember how Kafka had called the city a "dear little mother with claws" — I remember how my very normality was cause for suspicion — I remember as a child I was lost in maps, a magnifying glass in one hand and my heart in the other, as if I could follow the rumours of my parents through the Alps — I remember being told of a previously undetected mutation, a slight bend in the gene sequence, had occurred, which across the length of generations would turn significant, could set a family off course forever — I remember a public square where couples had gathered to dance to a violin and a man in the corner with a microphone and I remember this though I was not there — I remember a neighbour stirring a wooden broom handle in a burning trash barrel's leaf embers on his dark lawn, the blue Venetian lanterns blowing back against the shutters of the inn, the little town on the seacoast deserted as the hour swept in from the horizon — I remember wading into the sea, under the dark white expanse, a thousand needles of blue light from bioluminescent plankton and for the last time in my life I felt buoyant — I remember along a desolate road the massive electrical transmission towers leading into the city arose through the fog and started to hum — I remember from my father, whom in retrospect I would call X because nothing else fit, I had inherited a fascination for cartography and wariness of strangers — I remember his face surfacing through the water, developing like a Polaroid — I remember in those formative years, before I discovered writing, I hovered over the globe, as if a Fabergé egg whose surprise was a series of miniature family portraits which by winding a gear would unfold from a top hatch and click into place like a wing — I remember the promise of lyricism, which over years was reduced to a plain recounting of the facts and this left us in crisis, trapped in the hard architecture of the actual we ourselves had built, what had begun only as a single room to store our certainties like pressed flowers and ornate bottles of perfume we no longer wore but could not bring ourselves to discard when the essence was gone, and almost imperceptively this expanded until the conviction the here-and-now was all there ever was congealed into our new truth, that we would never love again, and so we stood in the window watching the snow cascading through the cedars for the fourth day and understood our failure was our unwillingness to see anything more than the acres of cold while wondering if the mailman, delayed in his rounds, would arrive fatigued at the door with a letter from elsewhere, a story, even a postcard we had sent to ourselves from Buenos Aires where we had never been —

New York City (lyric)

₪   The city doesn't have to make sense, it doesn't love you or anyone. And if you were to say, I have lived in your arms a long time and the view of the refinery fires is all I've ever dreamt of. And if you were to say that the soft glass of the Mies van der Rohe is a machine is an island is a time zone and that there are wolves in the park and see I love you mother would it matter to the Exxon station or the squatter's hut. And if you were to say these RGB sunsets over the rusting-shopping-cart pasture are going black and that surrealism is dead replaced by voicemail and the girl with the pink hula hoop you just imagined and the man counting the aeroplanes in their holding patterns wonders if they're Chinese. The city is not a collection of people, it's where we plant our antennas, the central node the roads lead from in eight directions. And if you were to say I am a bundle of vibrating strings and the city is in decline as an idea and on the time-elapsed film the mid-century apartment tower is taken apart like regret by unseen hands and in its dusty space sprout weeds and in its weeded space is melted gold. Moscow Caracas Budapest Tbilisi Yerevan my ears are ringing Kyoto São Paulo Microsoft Mandalay New York. And if you were to say our world will run out of air and if the sun breaks the windows at Sainte-Chapelle I am bathed in flames once more and if you were to say I separate the ineffable from the slave maker ant and confuse them again and I do this multiple times or my mind will atrophy in the blue suburban juntas and the dinner of onions and herring will grow cold in the cul-de-sac. The Well Wrought Urn holds the ashes of Baudelaire and the Rosa Mystica bleeding her aromatic oil on Palm Sunday offers her figure for your poems. And if you were to say the city in the visual static of a snowstorm in 1958 before the invention of the Taser and the metro entrance is an impromptu society of hats gathering for a journey to a nouveau resort. And if you were to say to the iron lung pushed through the streets you are more important than *Ulysses*. And if you were to say passer-by, cinema of lush flowers where you slept like Proust. The sky a perfect rectangle with a star nailed in each corner. Aoyama: year nine times the probability of grace is not enough. And if you were to say Hyderabad Favela Agora the sex workers in Lahore have gone on strike. And if you were to say, I hyperventilate into a brown sandwich bag when I read this. And if you were to say, what did you expect, bottles thrown from the roof.

Oslo, Winter 2011

₪   For two seasons, I was struck by migraines that would come without warning and with such extraordinary force the air would ripple in concentric circles pushing out from any light source. Often I would find myself on these occasions propelled backward into crowds on the sidewalk, which in a gesture of common humanity would catch me. And once whilst midway over a bridge in St. Petersburg, where I was intently focused upon an ephemeral white butterfly with three wings on a branch illustrated in a field guide I held as I walked, I heard a high-pitched whistling in the clouds turn into a roar with such a shock it catapulted me against the guardrail and shook loose scenes from an unremembered life that began to melt across the dome of my closed eyelids. My mother's flickering face downturned under a lamp as if refusing to be acknowledged, while with tweezers she carefully placed a pair of lashes, like two tiny spiders, into an envelope, the camera panning over a map of Europe, vignettes from a rugged seashore where in the grainy Mediterranean sunlight circa 1970 three women, beautiful but unfamiliar and incomprehensible to me, were laughing without any volume and when I opened my eyes I found the city had appeared to pause — the barge below loaded with blue Toyotas parting the stalled waters only now had begun to move again. As if repeatedly watching a film for details I might have missed, I would in subsequent years replay these scenes, but was panicked to find in this most unstable of mediums — memory — the scenes were degrading with each view, as if merely looking could set off a chemical corrosion that could not be reversed and would one day leave me with nothing more than a handful of rust-coloured powder for what was once life, captured. As I watched in my mind at night, I would zoom to inspect the delicate script on her envelope but would find it indecipherable or I would pause on a silhouette of a face on the wall to her left like a cameo (was it a lover's unannounced arrival?), or I would roam over a faded house in the lower frame that looked artificially aged. And the small oval floating in the back of the sky, no larger than a fennel seed, was a dirigible from which Italy was a single unbroken stem of a flower. Or had an atom of dust momentarily landed upon my eye, it was impossible to say. Each time I would recall these memories, the realities of where I was sitting, in the atrium of the Grand Palace Hotel in Berlin or on an aeroplane bound for New York, would calmly dissolve, leaving me with the sensation of being underwater and in the presence of something mysterious and protean, as if I were within an enormous school of sardines in the Aegean, swarming around me, turning from aluminum to black depending on the angle of the fluid geometries they formed and dispersed from instant to instant with each wave of my hand. When I think back to the other unaccountable hours in the grip of a migraine, time irretrievably lost except for a creased movie ticket or a hotel receipt for an unremembered sleep as evidence of my whereabouts in the arterial backwaters of a minor city where the black and white sky looked like a QR code, I recall how in the blotting pressure of those episodes I felt another consciousness attempting to access my own. In those days every keyhole, every telephone, every bottle of medicine glowed, as if lit with energy from within, the way ripe lemons are, and this led me to dwell on the inner radiance often found in saints depicted in medieval altarpieces or on the electrical fields of green light that envelope German children and livestock in the countryside during summer thunderstorms. In those days, I would fall silent at the apex of the pain when the tectonic plates of the past and present collided in my cerebellum and suddenly each man in the crowd erupting from the metro into the white noise of the city was my father, whose face had never been imprinted upon mine and thus could be anywhere, suddenly like an actor's began to appear whenever I hazarded a glance at a billboard or a side of a bus. The mere possibility of such an encounter made a monotonous life more urgent, and yet I ask, who does not want to be pursued, to be laid claimed to, knowing that one's existence was a matter of dire consequence for another? I would shield myself with an umbrella and depart into a stream of storefronts on Rue de Rivoli in the rain dropping pointillist dots on the sidewalk or slip into a bookstore and amongst the maze of shelves find a dusty and hidden corner favoured by amorous couples where I would begin scribbling notes on the back of a magazine retrieved at random, only to tear out the page as proof when I next awoke what had befallen me was not a product of my paranoid imagination, a fabricated world made from the things the mother brings and the things the father takes away. How else to restore those pirouettes of memory, hours walking the deslivered air? Thunder in the imagination. Those overwritten pages, where my writing rendered the print under them nearly illegible, were a ramble of words in ruins. That October, I relocated to the outer ring of Rome on a deserted street with a Poste Italiane and a crumbling osteria with irregular hours haunted by the owner, a man of sixty but already deep in the crow's autumn of regret from which few reemerge, who would watch football for hours on a silent monitor as the ceiling fan turned listlessly. I noted the lines etched on his ancient face were tributaries found on those who lost children at the onset of middle age. As if waiting for someone to appear out of elongated shadows of a forgotten past that kept growing, I watched what were seemingly the neighbourhood's only other residents, the widows who had taken the black in a show of devotion and were now, for all intents, married to each other. I would pass them in the fish market in the mornings and in the early evenings as they stared at me, like I was a rumour, as I made my way to the café, where I sat a week without relief before my journal, a failed clairvoyant with a flame and a circle of hair. Each nightfall, as the blue wind dropped on the villa's blank side, as in a de Chirico, a dozen Chinese garment workers, whom later I read were deported, filed noiselessly through the alley beneath my window. Each held a plastic bag orange as a floating lantern that I could see until the last of them turned a corner and was gone.

Prague, Summer 2010

ꔕ   In 2010 as my condition worsened and my gaze turned increasingly inward, curled like a nautilus, I began to worry I was ever more unfit for the world and that my Galápagos Syndrome had progressed to a stage whereby the internal chambers of my life into which I often retreated and the external forms (writing and speaking) by which I addressed myself to others were completely torqued together, utterly indistinguishable, so I had at last assumed the shape of my own introspection. I had become a creature that in spiraling fashion finds its own curiosity of interest. That summer, a doctor in Prague whom I consulted after a bout of narcolepsy had turned into seemingly incurable insomnia, informed me that I appeared to be, as he put it, "out of focus" and the excess fluid he detected around my eyes suggested I had become "submerged" within my own dreams, which as a result of my condition, no longer surfaced in sleep and had come to be a permanent feature of my waking life. He told me what I already knew of the mysterious connection between the mind and body that allows us to experience something simply by imagining it and told me he could do nothing except advise me in a series of guided imagery exercises he predicted would be to no avail. He recommended with a dismissal that I begin with a visit to the Kafka Museum on the Malá

Strana bank of the Vltava where I would find numerous photographs of the city's favourite son displayed beneath water in rooms painted with light-killing black, apparently in an effort to replicate a vision of the world that abhorred clarity. As I walked out of the Old Town that brisk morning in the general direction of the museum the sky contained a peculiar swirl of green one expects only on nights beyond the polar circles, a colour that caused the baroque statues guarding Charles Bridge to come alive in their silent, but saintly ecstasies, where they were hovering a few centimetres above each pedestal. It was then, as I remember it now, I came upon a set of crumbling stairs curling like a corkscrew and out of sight which seemed to take me an extraordinarily long time to descend, the noises of the city fading with each step that fell off into the air as I moved downward. As I held on to the makeshift rail, I felt I had greatly aged and could no longer walk without support. I was slowly moving through the space of this idea, contemplating how the weight of Prague's accumulated past meant a future here was almost unbearable, when to my disbelief I glimpsed a woman climbing out of the river onto the low mossy ledge with goggles still fastened about her face, her body steaming and cooling in wisps of smoke, as if a wax figure lifted from a

128

press that had just moulded her. I have always been transfixed by the sight of a woman the few precious seconds after she steps out of her bath, for the instant holds the prospect of two diverging narratives at the joint of their departure. The thought always ushered in the sensation of vertigo that even as a young boy would cause me to steady myself by placing a hand on the chair in the washroom, like a confused theatre-goer who walks in tardy to a play, the curtains drawn. Yet as I hesitated there on the last step, her hair tapering to a dark point like the lead of a pencil down her golden back and the Vltava's majestic lines dissolving soundlessly into the shadows of the bridge, I understood the utter impossibility of an alternate path in any story. This is especially true for the orphan: the death of one's mother is admission into a life consumed with her. The strange torpor I felt in the woman's presence was a sure sign, of my desire. But that, of course, did not register with her. She simply walked across the lawn of the thin riverside park, where she was greeted by another woman before they proceeded down a street on which the medieval guilds were once located and where, rumour has it, the King's alchemists once huddled over a fire of gold with a spoon of mercury. It was not until six months later I recalled the doctor's counsel regarding the Kafka Museum,

the memory triggered when I had become preoc-
cupied with a former escort, Ms. M., now a photo
retoucher in Berlin who had on her temple two tiny
scars like pale crescents in an alien sky, as I was once
told my dear mother had from scratching herself
in sleep. In fact, I often thought she was citing my
mother. She thought the scars made her unique and
when we made love would wear her fine hair like a
ribbon behind her ear so the scratches could be seen,
but knowing they were not original made her all the
more remarkable to me.

Oslo, Summer 2010

௫   Month by month things got worse, which in ret-
rospect was for the best. By the late summer of 2010,
my desire to travel to Barcelona to see the Museu
Sentimental bequeathed by the eccentric collector
of curiosities Frederic Marès took on the quality
of an obsession that began to impede my ability to
think clearly. Upon waking, I would devote a por-
tion of each morning to cataloguing the luminous
items that had appeared in my imagination the prior
night: Roman and Medieval keys laid out on red
velvet; scissors; hairpins fashioned from porcupine
spines; a taxidermied white rabbit in a bell jar; vases
encrusted with seashells, birds, wax fruit, insects, or
some combination of all; bills of exchange; licenses;
one hundred canes with handles scrimshawed with
the figures of reclining animals; mechanical dolls;
stereoscopes; magic lanterns to entertain in the eve-
ning; a nineteenth-century French table clock of
marquetry and gilded bronze but most notable for
its face with moving eyes; compact powders kept in
small embroidered purses, bouquet holders, mother-
of-pearl cameos, earrings made of peacock feathers,
decorative items from the feminine world of the
bourgeoisie for any event or emotion that may arise
unexpectedly, including mourning; miniature paper
theatres by the eighteenth-century engraver Martin

Engelbrecht featuring courtesans and the Massacre of the Innocents at Bethlehem; rows of daguerreotypes of the Catalan seaside, circa 1845, and of clergymen and artists with the kohl-eyed stare of the dead; battalions of colonial armies composed in tin; twelve lockets of curled hair — all sisters — preserved under glass. Which objects, these remnants of a departed man or woman, were in Marès's possession in the fortress of the Royal Palace of the Counts and which in the galleries of my sleep I had invented, I could never say, but the inability to draw the distinction, to tell for sure what was real and what was mere speculation, or which belonged to Marès on his shelves and in his cabinets and which were mine, if only as wisps of dreams in the lit-up neural circuitry in my brain where I held things I could not hold, was of little matter. In the depths of my fascination with Marès, when I was recuperating for several months on Halsnøy, I could be found most mornings as a fixture at the end of the pier, observing the deepwater fishing boats return through a blue antediluvian light on the horizon, nearly sinking under the weight of their nets quivering with trapped life hauled up from regions where submarines travelled. A few seagulls alert as centurions. A line of elderly women practicing tai chi, redirecting the ocean breeze around them like slow-moving fans. As I recall it now, I would wait nearly paralyzed with expectation when the nets dropped to the deck and spilled millions of translucent arctic krill, each with a thumbprint of fire near the head, crackling back and forth in a huge pile as if shocked with electricity. I remember in the hills behind me in a small apple orchard owned by the monastery where, for a modest fee and the promise of silence I was a welcomed guest, towered a thirty-foot statue of Our Lady of Grace whose arms, by some trick of the weather, were perpetually wrapped in clouds, though in the prior century she must have served as a lighthouse of sorts for boats that had lost their way. I cannot claim to comprehend the nature of this scene, but it has been burned permanently into my retina so that the ghostly afterimage of the Virgin reappears if I stare for too long at a white wall. In the film version of my life, I would have boarded the Thursday tour boat to Barcelona and on it met a middle-aged woman named Ms. Q. with a tiger-eye ring, the first thing I noticed, and one or two facts I learnt about her as we left the fjords behind was she had taken to living on the ocean and would not disembark when we arrived at the port and the palm trees and the possibilities of La Rambla. Because, she said, the enclosed and impeccably well-mannered society of the deck with nearly every personality and profession represented, together with the elliptical route of the voyage which amplified each moment while bringing time nearly to a standstill, so after awhile the conversations with the accountants from Milwaukee or the historians from Paris she had and the meals consumed during the prolonged fortnight, to say nothing of the open expanses of water upon which motion appeared to cease for days, or the sensation that the boat itself seemed to stay anchored in one place while the ocean moved around it until at last the narrow inlets and coves of Costa Brava filled with snorkelers appeared, were, she insisted, perfectly sufficient. What was to be gained, she said, if everyone will depart happy to return to a world precisely as they left it, unfamiliar and virtually incomprehensible? As we sat in silence before a plate of sardines flecked with parsley and grains of sea salt, I did not believe her, but wanted to. On the route back, she was nowhere to be found. In another life, I may have known her further, if only momentarily, but in the real world that I once thought held me captive, I came to understand over time and with the accumulated evidence each day provides that my recursive imagination and my desire to be free of a past that doubled back on itself like a serpent consumed with its own tail, were my true shackles. I had to learn to see the wonders and the loveliness of the base world before us as I broomed leaves and green flies turned up on their wings in the cloister's shaded arcades where I loitered at my duties prior to retiring to my cell. I would shut the door with the knowledge that the world was inside too, between the walls and the vaulted ceiling, and out of honour for it I would start to write minor notations I would never complete, the number of slate tiles on the floor (one hundred and forty-four), the spell for which the desktop's copper stain was illuminated by fading sunlight (nine minutes), the cobwebs weighted down with motes of dust, a whole universe lost every day — and upon closing my eyes on my cot I would recall the hooded monks singing the Liturgy of the Hours from earlier in the morning, beautifully together in their separation, and I would feel instantly and without fail as if I were being hoisted, suspended in my disbelief, on invisible strings toward the black ceiling slowly beginning to brighten with the first stars of evening.

Berlin, Summer 2011

ℶ   Through the chandeliered corridors upholstered in shadows and bevelled mirrors of the Grand Palace Hotel I walked in search of Ms. M., my footsteps keeping time with my pulse. Along the baroque frieze of angels in an arbor, under recessed ceilings painted in a trompe l'oeil of clouds, dark oils, rope tassels, voices on cellular phones retreating into an alcove, waiters and maids glimpsed briefly behind columns, into the atrium in which wind always blowing originated from nowhere. The fuel of all elegance and allegiance is delay. And so each time I caught sight of her descending the staircase, I contemplated the instant from every angle I could think of while still inside of it, even as I waited for the moment after, when the scene would be processed and filed away. The clink of her bracelet on marble, which catches the attention that has begun to wander, is followed by a close-up of the birthmark on her right ankle partially concealed by a strap so it appeared that censored letters in a seriffed font were peeking through. Had I approached through the columns of the eastern corridor, I would have noted that the point where the black seam of her dress expanded at her hip was her hand holding Marguerite Duras's *The Lover* and her pause on the stairs that coiled like a shell about to release her was due to the door revolving, though no one was in it. It rotated slowly, delivering from the outside voices of children, those who were about to depart, perhaps even her future self who, though gone, would continue to live on within her. Later on a bridge in St. Petersburg when I wondered if a butterfly has any instinctual recollection of its terrestrial life before the long, deep sleep of its transformation I knew the thought had come to me in a montage in which the final image was this one: her hem rustling in a light breeze was a shimmer of red. For what other reason than change in the midst of permanence did I see the world through a lens that would allow me to alter the sequence of events even if the knowledge gained was not that I knew her more, but understood myself less? Was that not the probable outcome of any true encounter, the kind that renders even the most familiar strange — a tree with all of its leaves removed? My encounters with women left me altered and perplexed not only by what I wanted, but also by the sheer notion of what it means to want. Years from now when (not if) I happen upon her again in this same hotel or another exactly like it, deserted but for the two of us, I will, despite my best intentions, have almost no point of reference except little ellipses of memory, the archipelago of my desires in the great wash of time. It is as if my desire, which by its very design cannot be fulfilled, has led me to perpetually build a new self around it while discarding the old shell. What stays with me is this: the beads of sweat I traced in a constellation of thoughts on her lower back while she read, the sun reaching its final efflorescence in the park. In retrospect, it was an image of tenderness we could agree upon from our half-dozen clandestine assignations. The road to the hotel was lined with conifers all the way to the horizon into which I stared as birds materialized in the sky, pouring out of a funnel in another dimension, so the whole tone of the afternoon darkened in an instant that would soon bring upon us a storm of beauty. Thus it came to be certain moments we shared, even if the sharing had been illusionary, carried extra weight that I refused to be divested of and would, in fact, infuse with more meaning I would retreat into as I sensed the very density of our encounters, however brief, were evaporating. Consider for instance the silk ribbon she purchased for pennies in an Indonesian market where the locals wore them around the wrist to curry favour with the gods of good luck and, curiously, as a reminder to forget the harms visited upon one in the prior year. She twisted hers into a question mark to bind her hair, which I unravelled by simply pulling on its loose thread and tied to the headboard as she drew the curtains closed and which now subsequently lost may indeed be used by the Dutch maid as a bookmark. I admit I can summon nothing of the original seller's face except her extraordinary blue eyeshadow that created the disturbing sensation that she was looking at me, even when her eyes were closed. The images — the Indonesian's eyes and Ms. M.'s — could not be spliced, but would remain, like horror and love, juxtaposed so the differences threw into distressing relief an underlying similarity. From the southern corridor of the hotel, an eye catches her attention so her hand slips as she looks left in mid-step on the stairs in Fibonacci's sequence, clinks the banister with her bracelet, while a waiter walks out of a mirror on the wall and the camera follows him through the hallway's telescoped arches receding in time all the way into the atrium balancing a tray of drinks, like a crystal city. Its refracted essence — a sensation of stillness and classical reassurance we could see through but like a Chardin painting believe in anyway. In this particular cut, I am in the corner taking notes on the two pale scars, like commas, on her temple and the graceful palm tree over my shoulder casts a shadow. Those whom fortune neglects is given a glimpse of something that surpasses all expectations, at least this is what I thought when I saw her leaving in the lunar, spectral light with her suitcase on whose right corner she had affixed an image of a nautilus cut away to display the whorled interior of its former life, the gloomy chambers marking a year at each turn and on whose left she had placed a decal of a fleur-de-lys and the French flag. In the hotel room, she turned and took two photographs: one of me striding across the carpet to her and the other of my hand on the lens. Out in the hallway, the wainscoting was carved with egrets, tropical flowers, colonial homes, a baroque frieze of angels, there were rumours of a garden, and the ceiling of clouds beginning to roil. I lay atop a florid duvet listening to her favourite music a year later and as I fell asleep I could feel dream liquid siphoned out of my brain through the coiled tubes of the headphones where a machine converted each drop into words in my journal. In my dream, she was at the same time as I in a high-ceiling room whose burgundy wallpaper had begun to peel and now formed a recursive loop with a damask pattern of leaves and pomegranates on the underscroll. Duras's book perched on her pillow like a bird, and as she slept completely enciphered in the perfect distributions of her body, she dreamt of me thinking of her, as if we were intertwined by a neural circuit in the suspended animation of sleep, its beautiful sentence that when it finally comes to an end drops us back onto the earth in a plume of dust. In my billfold is the out-of-focus photo of me crossing the room, the bed, the lamp, even the light from it elongated, streaks of energy emanating from all things stretched like a wire between two coordinates in space. It was evidence in the end of my wish to remain in the past and to be in the future simultaneously, which when overcorrected was certain to cause new issues in this attenuated life for the next lover, if there were to be one. The last time I saw her she was in a hat at dusk, looking like a woman about to board a train, and out of nowhere a shower of linden leaves. The streetlamps had come on but the air was still ignited with light, an ethereal quality as when you are awake inside a dream. I thought I could stand at this intersection for hours, the sun setting like a placebo. The effluvia of cars through the streets like lines of data. The sky was the colour of my anxiety. And pinned to her jacket a bou-tonnière — a dot in time that signaled a time beyond it — comprised of three small flowers arranged in a spiral of red, white, and yellow, a vertigo of enfolded petals that I gazed into until they began to spin.

Berlin, Late Fall 2011

囗 radaradaradaradaradaradaradaradaradarada-
radaradaradaradaradaradaradaradaradaradarada-
radaradaradaradaradaradaradaradaradaradarada-
radaradaradaradaradaradaradaradaradaradarada-
radaradaradaradaradaradaradaradaradaradarada-
radaradaradaradaradaradaradaradaradaradarada-
radaradaradaradaradaradaradaradaradaradarada-
radaradaradaradaradaradaradaradaradaradarada-
radaradaradaradaradaradaradaradaradaradarada-
radaradaradaradaradaradaradaradaradaradarada-
radaradaradaradaradaradaradaradaradaradarada-
radaradaradaradaradaradaradaradaradaradarada-
radaradaradaradaradaradaradaradaradaradarada-
radaradaradaradaradaradaradaradaradaradarada-
radaradaradaradaradaradaradaradaradaradarada-
radaradaradaradaradaradaradaradaradaradarada-
radaradaradaradaradaradaradaradaradaradarada-
radaradaradaradaradaradaradaradaradaradarada-
radaradaradaradaradaradaradaradaradaradarada-
radaradaradaradaradaradaradaradaradaradarada-
radaradaradaradaradaradaradaradaradaradarada-
radaradaradaradaradaradaradaradaradaradarada-
radaradaradaradaradaradaradaradaradaradarada-
radaradaradaradaradaradaradaradaradaradarada-
radaradaradaradaradaradaradaradaradaradarada-
radaradaradaradaradaradaradaradaradaradarada-
radaradaradaradaradaradaradaradaradaradarada-

radaradaradaradaradaradaradaradaradaradaradarada-
radaradaradaradaradaradaradaradaradaradaradarada-
radaradaradaradaradaradaradaradaradaradaradarada-
radaradaradaradaradaradaradaradaradaradaradarada-
radaradaradaradaradaradaradaradaradaradaradarada-
radaradaradaradaradarxxx

Berlin, Late Fall 2011

൬   I was pulled on a wagon through the snow through the gates of my demonic, postexilic city. And in the sky what I saw was fear and at the end a bright light in my face was there. Among the ruins was a radio that played one song. The subalterns huddled in rags under a freeway clover were the city's exorcized conscience. An alien presence in my mind kept speaking to me in a strange language about responsibility and love, which are harder to swallow than finely granulated bits of cement. Isn't this how it was meant to be: the long journey from happiness would start at the outskirts where the first apartment blocks formed a perimeter wall and there above you, tumbling up from the centre, a roaring whirlwind of a great green fire enfolding on itself, devouring the dark sky, and as your brain cracked with electricity you fumbled for the buttons on your shirt desperate to shed your clothing, when from an unfathomable depth of space rose the harmonious song of children that spread over the ice fields, a dawn chorus you continued to hear for the rest of your life? No, it would not be like this. Simpler, a mere residue of a former exuberance and flowered intricacy that could no longer be reconstructed. I was pulled on a wagon through my demonic, postexilic city, white in its luminous decrepitude like cocaine. Time had stopped moving as I moved through it. The original abattoir was no longer a dream but a diorama a child somewhere long ago had built in his garden. And I saw where the deracinated crowds had once slept in the public squares and with no respect for tradition had bathed in the fountains, splashing water on each other. The nude bodies reenacted a Roman mural destroyed by bleach and machete. These and other images would make their way into memory and later onto the pages of an eel-skin notebook. Everyone was gone, because I missed them. My catatonic father had not yet been born from his glass coffin. My dog looked back at me with something approaching regret and with fur smelling of the decay of seaweed. As I wrote, little flakes of skin fell off me. It was clear the Muslim in front of the hospital was an apparition or posthistorical. The sign pointed to a tombstone, then I surmised when I looked away the sign was a tombstone, not a birthing ward. The radio played one song loudly in a foreign language. It made the leaves rustle, but other than that, no effect. After two nights, a digression emerged in the road like a miracle. I passed it by because I didn't believe in it. The digression led to the sewer. I had a job to do. Nothing, not even fascination, could stop me. The bombers were painted with rainbows and given schoolgirls' names before they ascended into the nucleus of a dust-coloured cumulus cloud. I quickly went to sketch this in my book, that way I could refer to it later in the middle of the night, but it was already there altered. I sketched it over a drawing of a skyscraper concealed in fog. That was yesterday. A current of remorse moved through the city and could be heard even in sleep or when you placed two hands over your ears, screamed. I counted backward from zero until the numbers were imaginary and my tiny wagon stopped in front of a bank's window. It held an aquarium with an angelfish swimming around in circles with half its dorsal fin out of the evaporating water. It was inedible. Money was also useless because it was too dirty to eat and it burned too fast. Flowers filled the stomach. As I rode, two twin boys ran after asking *Are you my father? Are you my father?* My guilt metastasized in strange ways, sometimes as cancer, sometimes as an uncontrollable torrent of emotion that ended in marriage. The girl I loved was a mute and was never able to tell me she loved me, at least not in a way I could comprehend. I learnt to stop speaking with my hands. Whatever I touched fossilized. Look at the sorrow in this statue. The wagon rattled over cobblestone. Inside I loved my city, but it thought I was Jeremiah or a traitor. When the snow fell through the hole in the crumbling planetarium's dome, a curling, double-helixed smoke-trail of startled bats poured out into the skyline. I wrote these words too, but they were unsatisfying like the colour grey or lamb. The woman who would become my mother found me riding in a red wagon, just like this one, pulled through the streets by a sheepdog. When she lifted me into the sky for the first time, it was my primal scene, one I would spend my life trying to repeat for that same level of spontaneous wonder. Her face was brilliant, pixilated, and filled with a million crystals of ice. What I saw was fear, and bright, unholy fire in my eyes was there. She could see it too, even as she was holding her suitcase and once again as she lay dying. Neither the poets nor the doctors could help her pain. Even morphine was painful. In my demonic, postexilic city I had come to a calm decision or I had come to nothing, it was hard to tell which was which. My map was old, the edges turning back into bark and the ink into rivulets of water that washed off into my hand. Arrows pointed in several directions, which meant the city couldn't be summarized without turning into a foul blot. I pried one off and beneath it was another arrow's eroded shadow pointing the wrong way. Certainty is the result of a dead semiotics, and this would be true on any other day, even when your feet take you downhill to a small abandoned woodshop filled with toys. One day my father would be born and from that moment everything I owned would belong to him. My whole life, a simulacrum of a life elsewhere. *I was never much to begin with,* I saw these words written on my hand, by whom I don't know, but they seemed fitting enough for the moment, seemed to speak a certain wisdom that was hard to resist. I came to a point. The next street over might be called Violence, which with a turn and a number of switchbacks might lead to an elegy or maybe worse. Perhaps the structure was a series of multiplying crystals that we imagined on a clear morning, when we knew what we wanted, what we had to have more than all else, was taken from us. *Let's agree this is a purple maple, let's agree the city's reservoir is too polluted to swim in, let's agree the future car wreck will occur here, but the couple will by grace survive their wounds,* at some moment we said this, even if the words were never uttered. The war was unrequited, love had become a discourse too heavy to shoulder or bear alone. To give shelter. To keep. To love in secret but to stay moving, like sleepwalking, the body in the trance of the mind moving forward through an alley, a pocked wall outward to a court-yard's single bench yellow in the sodium light. I did not expect to find donkeys, but here was one trotting beside me, how funny and lackadaisical, as if this were the Kasbah and the denouement had already happened, which it had. Not even the poor could outlive the rapture, and so after pleasure was reduced to the shape of a key, who would inherit it, the land-fill, the paltry wristwatches, the stray dogs, or even this sick city, for my city of rotting horses, roses, remorse which in moments when I was faraway from myself in the furthest exile of sleep, I wept. I slept in the attic of a decaying A-frame that stood at a road's end like a monument to an alphabet no longer extant. The top window crested the branches, a widower's peak. And every day I surveyed the theatre of crum-bling buildings not ten kilometres away and watched the extraordinary dark colour of malaria settle each evening. When I felt most lost, I checked in my jour-nal to find where I was and how far I had come. The journal continued to write itself at the exact speed I read it. Logically, it could never predict my future whereabouts. It is easier just to have been lied to in your own language or to be truly wretched without the kindness attached. The last empty page could have been Marat's sordid bathtub, but to be blank! The city continued to unfold laterally in fractals for-ever under construction, each "such as" a river or a

158

tunnel or a telescope where, at the end, a corpse waited like a seed. If only I could carry all in my wagon. The radio ran out of music. I had no clue how long I had been travelling. Neither time nor distance mattered. Sleep seemed like the most natural response to the world, either that or killing yourself. I began to nod off to the gentle rhythm of the wheels, as I was pulled down a boulevard resplendent and blinking with Christmas decorations. So much depended on this one gesture, staying at ease until the event was over and all members had dispersed, reluctantly, and one awoke, not exactly refreshed, but neither sad, not yet. A remnant of a former loneliness. This story wasn't a circular one, for exile was now a form of asylum in the eternal present tense, which even birds sought. Something had brought me here, to a place where nothing ever happens, but nevertheless smells like it has been scrubbed with Clorox. I heard a whippoorwill whistle the sound of an O, followed by another O, and I looked up at the moon's tractor beam sucking dirt from the planet, and heard O, then a gunshot. A hole torn in the soft static in my ears. Everything said here is either accurate or true. I turned a page and saw my parents, because I had continued to read into dawn, were dead. The sun lifted through the unfinished architecture, the morning a kind of worked-for disappointment you can believe in, you can lay hold of. I sat there for a moment surrounded by abandoned cars. A pond materialised on the hillside, filled with light and a black swan.

Acknowledgments

I want to thank the editors of the following journals in which excerpts of *Moth; or how I came to be with you again* appeared, sometimes in different form: *Animal Farm, Another Chicago Magazine, Canary, Columbia: A Journal of Literature and Art, Columbia Poetry Review, Gulf Coast, The Missouri Review,* and *The Modern Review.*

My deepest gratitude to Carole Maso, Michael Martone, and Renee Gladman, and most especially to Sarah Gorham, Kirby Gann, Kristen Radtke, Megan Bowden, Jeffrey Skinner, and everyone at Sarabande who believed in this book and made it possible.

Chris Hosea

Thomas Heise is the author of *Horror Vacui: Poems* (Sarabande, 2006), *Urban Underworlds: A Geography of Twentieth-Century American Literature and Culture* (Rutgers University Press, 2011), and numerous essays. He is an Associate Professor at McGill University and lives in Montreal and New York City.